A TALE OF TWO CITIES

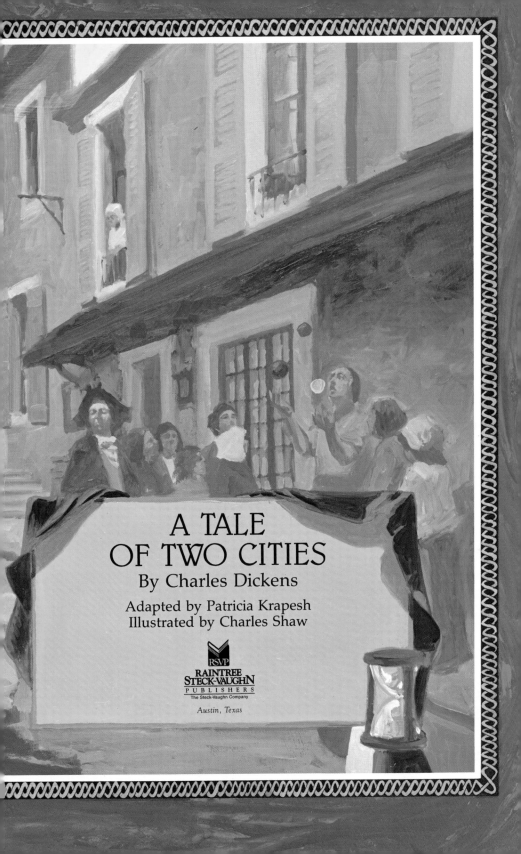

A TALE OF TWO CITIES

By Charles Dickens

Adapted by Patricia Krapesh
Illustrated by Charles Shaw

RSVP
RAINTREE
STECK-VAUGHN
PUBLISHERS
The Steck-Vaughn Company

Austin, Texas

Copyright © 1991 Steck-Vaughn Company

Copyright © 1980 Raintree Publishers Limited Partnership

Library of Congress Number: 79-24746

Library of Congress Cataloging-in-Publication Data

Krapesh, Patti.
  A tale of two cities.

  SUMMARY: Retells in simple vocabulary the classic tale
of the young Englishman who gives up his life during the
French Revolution to save the husband of the woman he
loves.
  1. France—History—Revolution, 1789-1799—Juvenile fiction. [1. France—History—Revolution, 1789-1799—Fiction.]
I. Dickens, Charles, 1812–1870. Tale of two cities. II. Shaw,
Charles, 1941–   III. Title.
PZ7.K85987Tal   [Fic.]   79-24746

ISBN 0-8172-1658-8 hardcover library binding

ISBN 0-8114-6840-2 softcover binding

  20 21 22 23 24 25 04 03 02 01

CONTENTS

RECALLED TO LIFE

1

It was the best of times, it was the worst of times, it was the age of wisdom, it was the age of foolishness . . .

On a foggy evening in the year 1775, Jarvis Lorry was on a mail coach headed toward Dover, England. The coach driver was nervous. The guard's loaded gun was on his lap.

"Tst! Joe!" cried the guard. "A horse at canter coming up. Yo there! Stand! I shall fire!"

"I have a message for a passenger — Mr. Jarvis Lorry," the rider said.

Mr. Lorry reassured the watchful guard. "There is nothing to fear. I belong to Tellson's Bank in London. I am going to Paris on business."

By the light of the coach lamp, Mr. Lorry read: "Wait at Dover for Mam'selle." To the messenger he said, "Say that my answer was RECALLED TO LIFE."

The next morning in Dover, Jarvis Lorry sat quietly at a breakfast table waiting for his meal. A bachelor of sixty years, he appeared to be a very orderly gentleman. When breakfast arrived he said to the waiter: "I wish a room prepared for a young lady who may arrive today, asking for a gentleman from Tellson's Bank."

Miss Manette arrived from London that evening. A pretty young lady of about seventeen, with golden hair and blue eyes, met Mr. Lorry's gaze with a questioning look.

"I received a letter from the Bank, sir, yesterday," she said with only a trace of an accent, "informing me that some discovery concerning my poor father — whom I never saw and who has been dead so long — would make it necessary for me to go to Paris to speak with a gentleman of the Bank. I asked permission to place myself under that gentleman's protection during the journey."

"I shall be more than happy to accompany you," said Mr. Lorry.

"Sir, I thank you. I was told that the business was of a surprising nature."

"It is very difficult to begin . . . Miss Manette, I am a man of business. I will tell you the story of one of our customers, a gentleman who was well known in Paris. I had the honor of knowing him there. At that time — twenty years ago — I worked in our French house of banking. The gentleman married an English lady and his business affairs were entirely in Tellson's hands."

"But, sir, this is my father's story," she said. "I was left an orphan when my mother died two years after my father's death. I was brought to England at that time."

Mr. Lorry guided Miss Manette to a chair. "As I was saying: the history of this customer is that he suddenly and silently disappeared; he was spirited away to an unknown prison; and his wife begged the King and the court for any tidings of him, and all in vain. The gentleman's wife wanted to save their child the pain she had felt. So she raised her daughter with the belief that her father was dead.

"Miss Manette, your mother took this course with you. And she left you at two years old to grow up without worrying whether your father soon wore his heart out in prison, or wasted there through many long years . . .

"My dear, your father has been found. He is alive. Greatly changed, though we will hope for the best. He has been taken to the house of an old servant in Paris, and we are going there. I, to identify him; you, to restore him to life, love, duty, rest, and comfort."

A shiver ran through Lucie Manette. "I am going to see his ghost — not him!"

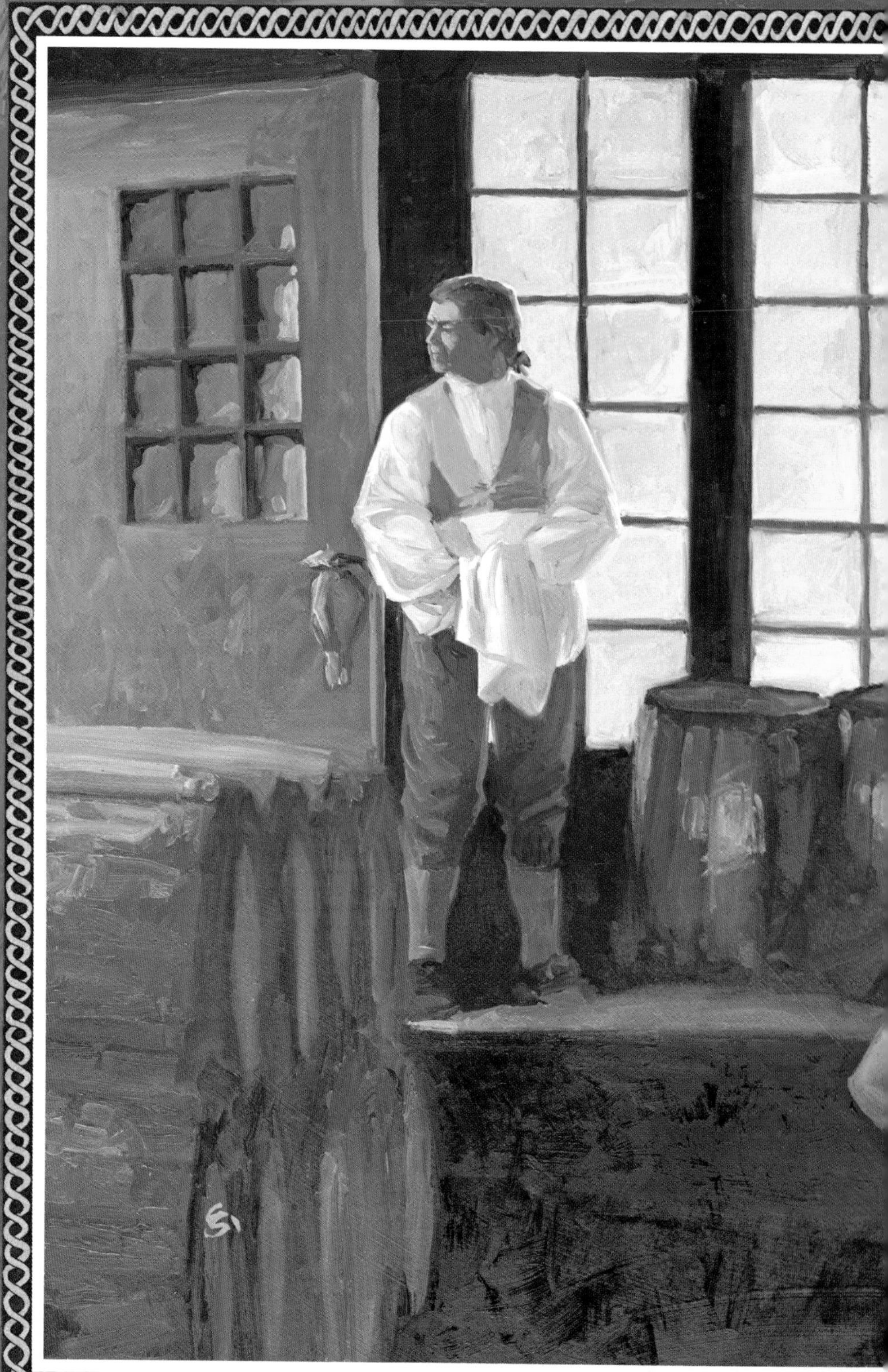

"There, there. You are well on your way to the poor wronged gentleman," Mr. Lorry said. "With a fair journey, you will be soon at his dear side.

"Only one more thing — he has been found under another name. His own is long forgotten, or long hidden. It would be dangerous to ask questions. It is better not to mention the subject and to take him out of France. I carry on me nothing referring to this matter. This is a secret service. My identity is all understood in the one line, 'Recalled to life;' which may mean anything."

The Paris in which Lucie Manette and Jarvis Lorry arrived was a city filled with many hungry and angry people. The aristocrats who ran the government had burdened the poor people with unfair taxes and laws. The injustices in France were such that a man could be tortured and executed for not bowing to a procession of monks.

In one part of the city, a wine cask had broken open and the deep red wine from inside it ran out onto the street. The people in the neighborhood celebrated briefly by scooping up the liquid with their hands and drinking it. One man used the wine to write the word "Blood" on a wall. Wineshop owner Ernest Defarge frowned and stepped back into his wineshop where Mr. Lorry and Lucie Manette sat waiting.

Madame Defarge, the wineshop keeper's wife, was a stout woman of about thirty. Her knitting was before her, but she had laid it down to pick her teeth with a toothpick. Mr. Lorry approached Monsieur Defarge, they spoke briefly, and Defarge went out. Mr. Lorry then beckoned to Lucie.

They joined Monsieur Defarge in a doorway which opened from a stinking little black courtyard. They reached the top of a foul-smelling stairway and Monsieur Defarge entered a darkened room. Before them sat a man on a low bench. With his back towards the door, he was stooping forward very busily making shoes.

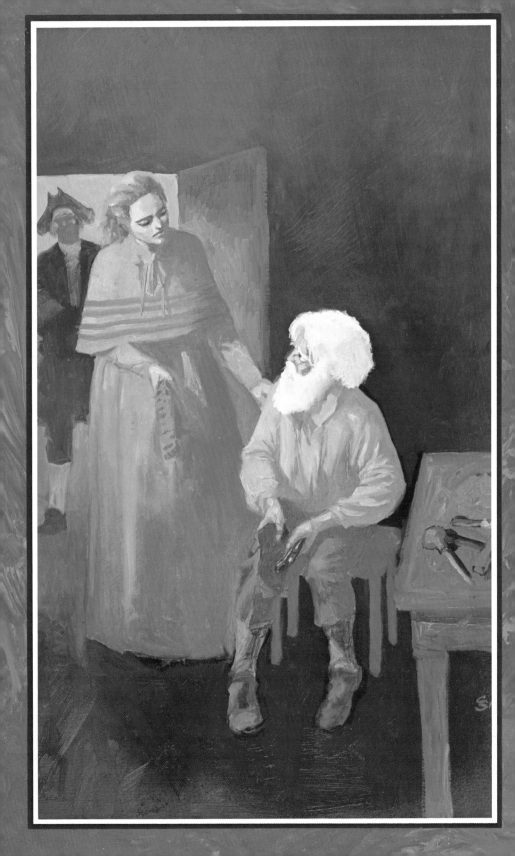

The door was opened further and a broad ray of light fell into the room, showing the workman pausing in his labor. He had a white beard, raggedly cut. Very bright eyes shone from his thin face which was capped by white, unruly hair. He put a hand up in front of his face to shield his eyes from the light.

"Tell us what kind of shoe it is," said Defarge.

"It is a young lady's walking shoe."

"And the maker's name?" said Defarge.

The shoemaker paused and said: "Did you ask me for my name?"

"Yes."

"One Hundred and Five, North Tower," said the shoemaker.

"Is that all?"

"One Hundred and Five, North Tower," he repeated.

Lucie Manette moved closer to his bench. He stared at her with a fearful look and asked, "Who are you?"

She sat down beside him. "O, sir, at another time you shall know my name, and who my mother was, and who my father was."

When Mr. Lorry and Monsieur Defarge left the room to make preparations for the journey back to England, Lucie's father was in her arms with his head resting peacefully against her shoulder. Later in the day the four descended the stairs.

In the courtyard only Madame Defarge was to be seen. She leaned against the doorpost, still knitting.

FIVE YEARS LATER

2

Five years later, Mr. Lorry was in the Old Bailey in London where a trial for treason was taking place. The punishment for treason was a violent death. Curious onlookers excitedly waited to see the prisoner.

The judge entered and the prisoner — a handsome gentleman about twenty-five years old — was brought in. The prisoner Charles Darnay had pleaded not guilty to a charge that he had helped the King of France in wars against England and was therefore a traitor.

The Attorney General, a court official, told the jury of bewigged gentlemen that the prisoner had often passed between France and England on secret business. The Attorney General praised the patriotic English citizen — John Barsad — who had brought the prisoner's traitorous actions to the attention of the court.

Another court official stood to question the patriot. Had he — John Barsad — ever been a spy himself? No. Ever been in prison? Certainly not. Never in a debtor's prison? Didn't see what that had to do with it. Never? Yes. Ever borrow money of the prisoner? Yes. Ever pay him? No. No motives but motives of sheer patriotism? None whatever.

The Attorney General called Mr. Jarvis Lorry to answer questions. "Mr. Lorry, on a Friday night in November 1775, did you travel between London and Dover by coach?"

"I did."

"Was the prisoner one of the other passengers?"

"I cannot say. The night was so dark."

"Have you seen the prisoner before?"

"When I was returning from France, the prisoner came on board the ship in which I returned to England."

Then the official called Miss Manette.

"Have you seen the prisoner before?"

"Yes, sir, on the same occasion as Mr. Lorry."

"Had you any conversation with the prisoner?"

"Yes, sir," she faintly continued, "he noticed that my father was in a very weak state of health. He expressed great gentleness and kindness for my father's condition, and I am sure he felt it."

"Had he come on board alone?"

"No, two French gentlemen were with him until it was time for them to leave the ship."

"Had any papers been handed about among them?"

"Yes, but I don't know what papers."

"Now to the prisoner's conversation, Miss Manette — "

"The prisoner was kind and helpful to my father. I hope," she said bursting into tears, "I may not repay him by doing him harm. He told me he was travelling on business of a delicate nature. He said this business might take him between France and England for a long time to come."

The purpose of the questioning was to prove that five years ago the prisoner had traveled in the Dover mail coach, and after leaving it passed secret information to another spy.

During the questioning, another wigged gentleman in the courtroom wrote a word or two on a piece of paper and tossed it to the man defending Charles Darnay.

Suddenly the prisoner's counsel addressed John Barsad. "You say again you are quite sure that it *was* the prisoner who passed on secret information?"

The witness was quite sure.

"Did you ever see anybody very like the prisoner?"

"Not so like him that I could be mistaken."

14

"Look well upon that gentleman." He pointed to the man who had written the note. "Then look well upon the prisoner."

Aside from the fact that the other man's appearance was careless and untidy, they were enough like each other to surprise, not only the witness Barsad, but everybody present. The likeness grew more remarkable when the other man removed his wig.

If he had made a mistake once, he could make it twice, said the counsel.

The similarity of Mr. Sydney Carton to the prisoner Charles Darnay was all that the counsel for Darnay needed to destroy the witness's testimony.

The trial had lasted all day and the lamps in the court were being lighted when the jury returned their decision. Charles Darnay was *not* guilty of treason.

Lucie, Doctor Manette, Mr. Lorry and others gathered round Charles Darnay and congratulated him. Darnay kissed Lucie's hand gratefully.

Dr. Manette appeared tired and strained. His face had become frozen in a very curious look at Darnay, deepening into a frown of dislike and distrust, mixed with fear.

"Shall we go home, Father?" asked Lucie.

With a long breath he answered, "Yes."

Mr. Lorry departed and Sydney Carton appeared out of the shadows. "This is a strange chance that throws you and me together," he said to Darnay.

They walked to a tavern where Charles Darnay ate and Sydney Carton drank wine. Sydney Carton was a strange man. He seemed to have lost all interest in living. During their conversation, Carton said bitterly: "As to me, the greatest desire I have is to forget that I belong to this world."

"You and I are not much alike in that respect," said Darnay.

"Now your dinner is done," Carton said later, "why don't you give a toast?"

"Miss Manette," said Charles Darnay.

"Miss Manette," echoed Sydney Carton.

"That's a fair young lady," Carton added. "How does it feel to be the object of such sympathy and compassion, Mr. Darnay?"

Darnay answered not a word, but he thanked Carton for aiding him during the trial.

"It was nothing to do in the first place," Carton said, "and I don't know why I did it, in the second."

After paying the bill, Charles Darnay rose and wished Sydney Carton good night.

"A last word, Mr. Darnay: you shall know why I drink. I am a disappointed drudge, sir. I care for no man on earth, and no man cares for me."

"Much to be regretted," Darnay replied. "You might have used your talents better."

"Maybe so, Mr. Darnay. Good night!"

MONSEIGNEUR AND NEPHEW

3

Monseigneur, one of the great lords in power at the Court of France, held a reception every two weeks in his grand hotel in Paris.

Following this reception, one Court member went down into the courtyard, got into his carriage and was driven away. He was about sixty, well-dressed, and haughty in manner. There was a look of cruelty about his handsome face.

The carriage dashed through the narrow streets and swept round corners, with women screaming before it, and men clutching children out of its way. Swooping around a street corner, one of its wheels came to a sickening jolt. There was a loud cry from many voices, and the horses reared and plunged.

"What has gone wrong?" said the Monseigneur impatiently.

"Pardon, Monsieur the Marquis!" said a ragged and timid man, "it is my child."

The Marquis St. Evrémonde ran his eyes over the crowd of people and took out his purse. "It is extraordinary to me," said he, "that you people cannot take care of yourselves and your children. How do I know what injury you have done my horses?"

He threw out a gold coin. And one onlooker said, "Be a brave man, my Gaspard! It is better for the poor little plaything to die so, than to live. It has died in a moment without pain. Could it have lived an hour as happily?"

"And who are you?" said the Marquis.

"They call me Defarge. I am a vendor of wine."

The Marquis threw a gold coin to the wine vendor and instructed, "Spend it as you will." Monsieur the Marquis leaned back in his seat and was just being driven away when a coin flew into his carriage, and rang on its floor. "Hold!" said the Marquis.

He looked to the spot where the wine vendor had stood, but the only figure standing there was a dark stout woman, knitting. "You dogs," said the Marquis, "I would ride over any of you very willingly, and exterminate you from the earth."

He leaned back in his seat again and the carriage moved on.

Riding from Paris to the Evrémonde country estate, the Marquis passed through countryside where both the crops and the people were poor and withered. When the carriage stopped, the great door of his château was opened by a servant and the Marquis asked, "Has Monsieur Charles arrived from England?"

"Not yet, Monseigneur."

Inside the Marquis' Château a supper-table for two was laid. The Marquis was more than halfway through his dinner when his nephew — known in England as Charles Darnay — arrived.

Darnay, who was not on good terms with his uncle, was soon saying gloomily to the Marquis, "We have so asserted our station that I believe our name to be more hated than any name in France."

"Repression is the only thing that lasts. The dark respect of fear and slavery," observed the Marquis, "will keep the dogs obedient. I will keep the honor of this family if you will not."

"Our family's honor is important to both of us, in different ways," the nephew replied. "Even in my father's time — which is equally yours — we did a world of wrong, injuring every human creature who came between us and our pleasure."

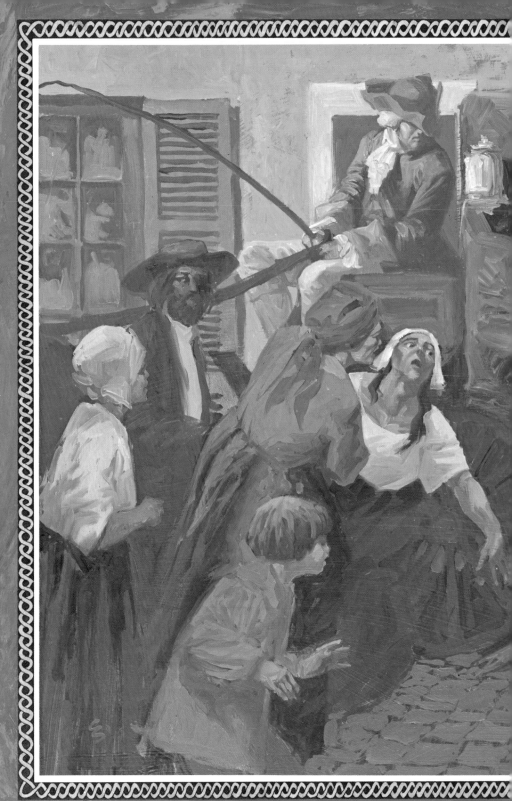

"I am bound to a system that is frightful to me," Darnay said, "responsible for it, but powerless in it. I am seeking to fulfill the last request of my dear mother's lips, which begged me to have mercy and correct the wrongs of this family. This property and France are lost to me. I am giving them up." And Darnay left the house that night.

The following morning when the sun was still low in the sky, people could be heard running quickly up and down the stairs. The cause of all the activity was a dead figure on a bed pillow. Driven into the heart of the Monsieur the Marquis was a knife with paper attached to it, on which was scrawled:

"Drive him fast to his tomb. This from JACQUES.*"*

A year after the trial, Charles Darnay was living in England as a teacher of the French language and French literature. He had loved Lucie Manette from the hour of his danger and time of the trial, but he had never spoken to her about these feelings.

One summer day he called on the Doctor, knowing that Lucie would be out. During their conversation Charles said, "Dear Doctor Manette, I love your daughter devotedly. If ever there were love in the world, I love her."

Doctor Manette sat silent, with his face bent down. His breathing was a little quickened as he spoke mournfully, "I have thought so before now. I believe you."

"Doctor Manette, like you, I have voluntarily left France because of its oppressions and miseries. Like you, I have chosen to earn a living away from it. I do not wish to take Lucie away from you as your child, companion, and friend, but to bind her closer to you, if such a thing can be."

"I believe your object to be as you have stated it. If she should ever tell me that she loves you, I will give her to you. She is everything to me; more to me than suffering, more to me than wrong, more to me — "

So strange was the fixed look upon his face, and the way in which he faded into silence, that Darnay felt uneasy. "I

22

wish to confide in you, Doctor Manette. My present name is not, as you will remember, my own. I wish to tell you what that is, and why I am in England."

"Stop!" said Doctor Manette. "Promise that you will tell me when I ask you, not now. Give me your hand. She will be home directly, and it is better she should not see us together tonight. Go! God bless you!"

Sydney Carton had visited the Manette home often during the year. One day he called on Lucie and found her alone. Looking into his sad face, she said, "I fear you are not well, Mr. Carton!"

"No, but the life I lead, Miss Manette, is not a healthy one."

Looking gently at him, she was surprised and saddened to see that there were tears in his eyes. There were tears in his voice too, as he said:

"It is too late to change. I shall never be better than I am. I shall sink lower and be worse. Miss Manette, I wish you to know that you have been the last dream of my soul. The sight of you with your father has stirred old shadows that I thought had died out of me. Since I have known you, I have had unformed ideas of beginning anew and trying to lead a better life.

"The utmost good that I am capable of now, I have come here to talk to you about. Let me carry through the rest of my misdirected life, the remembrance that I opened my heart to you, and that there was something left in me at this time which you could pity."

He was so unlike what he had ever shown himself to be; and Lucie Manette wept mournfully for him. "Be comforted," he said, "I am not worth such feeling, Miss Manette. An hour or two from now, I shall be as you have seen me before.

"The last thing I beg of you is this — for you, and for any dear to you, I would do anything. Think now and then that there is a man who would give his life, to keep a life you love beside you!"

FIRE RISES

4

Madame Defarge was pouring wine when Monsieur Defarge, with another man, entered the wineshop. "My wife," said Defarge, "I have travelled a long distance with this man called Jacques. Give him a drink."

Soon Defarge and the man called Jacques departed. They entered a room where there were three other men. Defarge closed the door carefully and spoke in a subdued voice:

"Jacques One, Jacques Two, Jacques Three! This is the witness met by me, Jacques Four. He will tell you all. Speak, Jacques Five!"

Jacques Five told the story of Gaspard, the man whose child was run down and killed by the Marquis St. Evrémonde. Gaspard had murdered the Marquis for revenge and then had gone into hiding for several months. Jacques Five told the other members of the Jacquerie (the men who all called themselves Jacques) how Gaspard was finally captured and hanged.

"How you say, Jacques?" demanded Number One. "Shall the Evrémonde château and all the inheritors be listed as doomed to destruction?"

"The château and all the race," returned Defarge. "Extermination."

"Are you sure," asked Jacques Two, of Defarge, "that no embarrassment can rise from our manner of keeping the register?"

"Jacques," returned Defarge, "if my wife undertook to keep the register in her memory alone, she would not lose a word of it. Knitted in her own stitches and her own symbols, it will always be plain to her and to us only."

Some days later, Monsieur and Madame Defarge learned that another spy had been commissioned for their part of the city — an Englishman named John Barsad. The next day the spy Barsad went to Defarge's wineshop. In the course of a conversation with Monsieur Defarge, John Barsad said, "When Doctor Manette was released, you, his old servant, had the charge of him. I have known Doctor Manette and his daughter in England. Yes, Miss Manette is going to be married," Barsad continued, "to one who, like herself, is French by birth. It is a curious thing that she is going to marry the dead Marquis St. Evrémonde's nephew who lives unknown in England. But he is no Marquis there, he is Mr. Charles Darnay."

Barsad soon left and Monsieur Defarge said to his wife, "I hope for Lucie Manette's sake that destiny will keep her future husband out of France."

"Her husband's destiny," said Madame Defarge, "will take him where he is to go, and will lead him to the end that is to end him." She continued knitting and Charles Darnay's name was added to the others on her register.

The day had come when Charles spoke to Lucie of marriage, and she spoke to her father for his permission. With great happiness they were married, and lived with Dr. Manette.

In 1789, Lucie and Charles Darnay had been married eight years and had a daughter named Lucie. Doctor Manette and Charles had successful careers; and some half-dozen times a year, at most, Sydney Carton visited the home where the four lived together.

The scene was not so peaceful in Paris. Led by the Defarges and the Jacquerie, the citizens had armed themselves to attack the Bastille. Madame Defarge was not knitting this day. In her right hand was an axe instead of a knitting needle, and in her girdle were a pistol and a cruel knife.

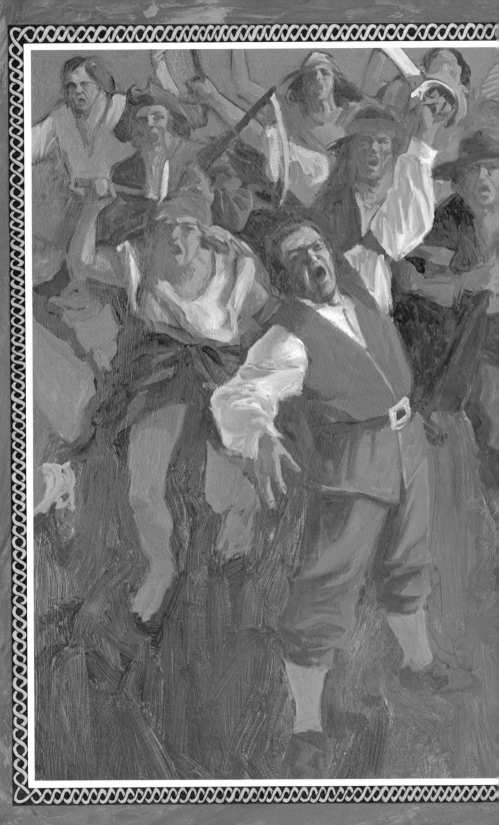

"Come then!" cried Defarge, in a resounding voice. "Patriots and friends! The Bastille!"

Once inside the prison, Defarge laid his hand upon one of the jailers. "Show me the prison cell, One Hundred and Five, North Tower. Quick!"

The jailer took him to the cell. "Pass that torch slowly along these walls, that I may see them," Defarge ordered.

Then shortly, "Stop!" he said. "The initials A.M.," (he spoke to himself) "Alexandre Manette. And here he wrote 'a poor physician.' "

Defarge searched the prison cell and returned to the courtyard where the patriots were shouting and rushing about.

At the day's end the governor who had defended the Bastille was slaughtered; seven prisoners had been rescued; and the heads of seven prison guards were displayed on spears.

That same night, in the village near the Evrémonde estate, the people had eaten their poor suppers, but did not creep to bed as usual. They gathered at the village fountain and whispered and looked expectantly at the sky in one direction only. Monsieur Gabelle — a villager who had worked for the dead Monseigneur — became uneasy, climbed to his housetop, and looked in that direction too.

The night deepened. And presently in the direction of their stares the château, formerly occupied by Monseigneur Evrémonde, was growing bright. The flames soared to the sky.

"Help, everyone!" The village alarm bell rang impatiently but the people stood with folded arms looking at the pillar of fire in the sky.

The château burned and Gabelle, whose job had to do with the collection of rent and taxes, hid behind a stack of chimneys on his housetop. The villagers pounded on his door throughout the night, but by dawn they were gone. Gabelle came down from his housetop, bringing his life with him for that while.

IN SECRET

5

One August day in 1792, Charles Darnay and Mr. Lorry were having a conversation at the latter's desk in Tellson's Bank. The elder man was explaining that he was leaving for France that evening to tend to Tellson's banking house in Paris. Mr. Lorry was interrupted when someone carrying a soiled and unopened letter asked if he had yet discovered any trace of the person to whom it was addressed. The man laid the letter down close to Darnay, who quickly recognized his own French name. The address, turned into English, ran:

"Very pressing. To Monsièur Marquis St. Evrémonde, of France. Confided to Tellson and Co., Bankers, London, England."

"No one can tell me where this gentleman is to be found," Mr. Lorry was telling the man.

On the morning of Lucie and Charles' wedding, Charles had told Doctor Manette his real name. The Doctor's reaction, which puzzled Charles, was horror and fear, and he requested of Charles that no one — not even Lucie — should ever be told of his real name. Charles had kept the promise.

Recalling this, Charles said to Mr. Lorry, "I know the fellow. I will deliver the letter to him."

Feeling very ill at ease, Charles went to a private place and read the letter.

MONSIEUR THE MARQUIS:

After having long been in danger of my life at the hands of the village, I have been violently seized and brought to Paris. The crime for which I shall lose my life is treason against the people of the Republic, in that I have acted against them for a refugee. I have explained to my jailers that I acted for them, according to your commands that no rent be collected and the people be spared any further oppression. My jailers' only response was that I had acted for an emigrant — a refugee from France — and where is that emigrant? I cry in my sleep where is that emigrant? I beg you to sympathize and release me. My fault is that I have been true to you. I pray you be true to me!

Your afflicted,

GABELLE

Through written instructions at an earlier time, Charles had told Gabelle to spare the people, to give them what little there was to give. Faced with this appeal by Gabelle, an innocent prisoner, Charles decided to go to Paris. He truly believed that he would be in no danger because he had voluntarily given up his estate.

That night he wrote two letters. One was to Lucie, explaining his strong need to go to Paris and reassuring her that he would be in no danger. The other was to the Doctor, leaving Lucie and their child in his care and reassuring him also that a safe return would be made.

The next evening, after embracing Lucie and pretending that he would return by-and-by, he left to begin his journey. He gave the two letters to a trusty messenger to be delivered late that night.

After traveling very few days of his journey in France, Charles realized there was no hope of return until he was declared a good citizen at Paris. Every town-gate had its

band of citizen-patriots who inspected travelers' papers and turned them back, sent them on, or jailed them.

One evening Charles stopped in a little town still a long way from Paris. Nothing but the presentation of Gabelle's letter would have got him so far. This same night he was awakened by two armed patriots in rough red caps with tricolored cockades.

"Emigrant," growled one patriot, "we are escorting you to Paris."

When Charles at last arrived at Paris, with an escort on each side, the barrier to the city was strongly guarded.

Charles looked around and saw that getting into the city was easy enough for peasants' carts bringing in supplies, but leaving the city for anyone was very difficult. The red cap and tricolor cockade were universal, both among men and women.

Charles was conducted into the guard room. An officer with a dark expression said, "You are sent, Evrémonde, to the prison of La Force."

"Under what law, and for what offence?" exclaimed Darnay.

"We have new laws, Evrémonde, and new offences," the officer said with a hard smile.

Another man motioned for Charles to follow him. "It is you," this man said in a low voice as they went down the guardhouse steps, "who married the daughter of Doctor Manette, once a prisoner in the Bastille. My name is Defarge."

"My wife came to your house to reclaim her father," Charles replied. "Will you help me? I must get word to Mr. Lorry of Tellson's — "

"I will do," Defarge interrupted, "nothing for you. My duty is to my country and the people. I am the sworn servant of both, against you."

At the prison called La Force, Charles was shocked by the sight of the many aristocratic prisoners who looked so out of place in their surroundings. There was a murmur of sympathy from them as he crossed the room.

Charles was led up a stone staircase and into a solitary cell.

In Paris, Mr. Lorry was sitting by a newly lighted fire when the gate bell sounded and the door suddenly opened. Lucie and Doctor Manette rushed in. They quickly explained that they had come to Paris when they had learned that Charles was imprisoned at La Force.

In a short while, Mr. Lorry asked to speak with Doctor Manette alone. A mob of people were gathered outside in the courtyard sharpening their knives on a grindstone which had recently been moved there. "They are murdering the prisoners," Mr. Lorry whispered.

Doctor Manette, a former inmate of the Bastille, felt certain that they would not harm him; so he went out into the mob to talk to them. In a few minutes, Mr. Lorry saw the mob surround Doctor Manette. Then suddenly the group hurried away with cries of "Live the Bastille prisoner! Help for the Bastille prisoner's kindred in La Force! Save the prisoner Evrémonde!"

Mr. Lorry hastened to Lucie. He told her that her father was helped by the people and had gone in search of Charles.

The next evening Monsieur Defarge delivered a message to Mr. Lorry from Doctor Manette. It read:

Charles is safe, but I cannot safely leave this place yet. The carrier of this message has a short note from Charles to his wife. Allow him to deliver it.

Mr. Lorry took Defarge to the lodgings which he had found that day for Lucie and the Doctor. Defarge had asked that his wife go with him so that she could identify Lucie and protect her.

The threesome found Lucie with her child. Lucie read Charles' note:

DEAREST —

Take courage. I am well, and your father has influence around me. Kiss our child for me.

"Is that his child?" said Madame Defarge, pointing her knitting-needle at little Lucie. A dark and threatening shadow seemed to fill the room. "It is enough," said Madame Defarge. "I have seen them."

She resumed her knitting and they left.

Doctor Manette did not return for four days. During that time, eleven hundred defenceless prisoners of both sexes and all ages were killed. The Doctor announced himself by name and profession and told of his eighteen years in the Bastille. He begged the self-appointed Tribunal to free Charles Darnay. When they refused, he pleaded to stay inside the prison with his son-in-law to assure his safety.

Though the Doctor tried hard to get Charles set free, the new era of the Republic of Liberty, Equality, Fraternity, or Death had begun. The King and Queen were tried, doomed, and beheaded. Above all, one hideous figure grew familiar — the instrument of death called La Guillotine. In twenty-one minutes one morning, the heads of twenty-one people of high public mark were lopped off.

Among these terrors, the Doctor walked with a steady head, never doubting that he would have Lucie's husband returned to her. The Doctor had been made the inspecting physician of three prisons, including La Force. He saw Charles weekly and was able to carry messages from him to Lucie.

Time swept by and Charles had lain in prison one year and three months. During all that time, Lucie was never sure, from hour to hour, but that the Guillotine would strike off her husband's head the next day.

One snowy December day, Doctor Manette told her, "Charles is summoned tomorrow for his trial. My darling, he shall be returned to you within hours."

ON TRIAL

6

Looking at the jury and the turbulent audience on the day of his trial, Charles might have thought that the criminals were trying the honest men. The lowest, cruelest, and worst populace were the directing spirits of the scene. Charles was accused by the public prosecutor of being an emigrant. "Take off his head!" cried the audience.

The questioning began and Charles explained that he had given up his inheritance and moved to England, where he earned his own living as a teacher.

Doctor Manette was questioned next. His personal popularity and the clearness of his answers made a great impression. He said Charles Darnay was always faithful and devoted to his daughter and himself in their exile. This carried more force than anything else revealed. Finally the jury declared they had heard enough and were ready to vote.

At every vote, the audience shouted and applauded. All votes were in the prisoner's favor. The President declared him free and the crowd swarmed about Darnay, put him in a great chair, and carried him home.

The next evening Lucie and Doctor Manette heard a knock at the door and four rough men in red caps, armed with sabers and pistols, entered. They said they were there to arrest Charles Darnay on new charges. One of the men told Doctor Manette, "He is denounced by the Citizen and Citizeness Defarge. And by one other."

"What other?"

"Do *you* ask, Citizen Doctor? You will be answered tomorrow."

Dr. Manette's family was unaware of two new arrivals in Paris; Sydney Carton, who had come to stay with Mr. Lorry, and the spy John Barsad. Carton had heard of Lucie's trouble. When he saw Barsad in a wineshop, a plan formed in his mind.

Barsad turned pale when he saw Carton, knowing he could be denounced as an English spy.

"Do you have keys to the prison?" asked Carton.

"I do sometimes."

"Come into the room here, and let us talk alone."

When they finished talking, Sydney Carton walked to a nearby chemist's shop. Inside the shop, he laid a scrap of paper before the owner. Certain small packets were made and given to him; he paid for them and left.

Morning arrived and Sydney Carton went to the place of the trial. Mr. Lorry was there, and Lucie was seated beside her father.

The trial began and the public prosecutor announced Darnay's accusers. "Ernest Defarge, wine vendor. Thérèse Defarge, his wife. Alexandre Manette, physician."

Doctor Manette turned pale and trembled. He denied having denounced Charles Darnay, but was told to be silent; and Defarge was called to explain.

The day that the Bastille was taken Defarge had searched the cell known as One Hundred and Five, North Tower where Doctor Manette had been imprisoned. "In a hole in the chimney, I found a written paper in the handwriting of Doctor Manette."

The paper was read:

"I — ALEXANDRE MANETTE, unfortunate physician — write this melancholy paper in my doleful cell in the Bastille, during the last month of 1767."

The Doctor described a night in 1757 when two cloaked men commanded him to get into their carriage because his

services as a doctor were needed. They took him into the country to an estate.

"The patient was a beautiful woman, not much past twenty. Her eyes were wild, and she constantly uttered piercing shrieks, and repeated the words, 'My husband, my father, and my brother!' "

He gave her medicine and learned there was another patient: " . . . a peasant boy, not more than seventeen, who was dying of a wound from a sharp point."

Doctor Manette asked the twins for an explanation. " 'A crazed young common dog! A serf!' said one of the twins. 'He forced my brother to draw upon him with a sword.' "

"Then the boy spoke. 'Doctor, they are very proud, these nobles; but we common dogs are proud too.

" 'We were tenants,' the boy continued, 'of that man who stands there. The other is his brother. My sister had not been married long when that man's brother saw and admired her, and asked that man to lend her to him — for what are husbands among us! The brother agreed, but my sister was good and virtuous and hated both the brothers.

" 'You know, Doctor, it is among the rights of these nobles to harness peasants — like dogs — to carts, and drive us. They did this to my sister's husband. It is also among their rights to keep us in their grounds all night, quieting the frogs, so that their noble sleep may not be disturbed. They kept my sister's husband in the unhealthy mists at night, and put him back into harness in the day. One day, at noon, he died in my sister's arms. Then, with that man's permission and aid, his brother took my sister away for his brief pleasure.

" 'When I took the tidings home, our father's heart burst and he died. I took my younger sister to a place beyond the reach of this man. Then I tracked the brother here and climbed in, sword in hand. He came in and tossed me some pieces of money. But I struck at him to make him draw his sword.'

"The dying boy turned to the brother and said, 'Marquis, in the days when all things are to be answered for, I sum-

40

mon you and your bad race to answer for them. I mark this cross of blood upon you.' He motioned in the air and died. The young woman died a week later."

When Doctor Manette returned home he wrote a letter to the Court, reporting what had happened. Before he delivered it, a woman visited him.

"The young lady was engaging and handsome, but not marked for long life. She was very troubled and presented herself to me as the wife of the Marquis Saint Evrémonde. She had learned of her husband's part in his twin brother's cruelty to the peasant girl and her family.

"She was a good, compassionate lady. When I walked her out there was a boy, two or three years old, in her carriage.

" 'For his sake, Doctor,' she said in tears, 'I will do all I can to make amends. I will make it the charge of his life to help this injured family, if the sister can be discovered.'

"She kissed the boy, and said, 'Thou wilt be faithful, little Charles?' The child answered her bravely, 'Yes!'

"Later that night, a man rang at my gate, demanded to see me, and followed my youthful servant Ernest Defarge upstairs where I was. The man said it was an urgent case, and I was taken to a carriage. Then, as I had feared, twin brothers crossed the road from a dark corner. The letter I had written, which was in my pocket, was taken from me, and I was brought here to the Bastille, to my living grave.

"I, Alexandre Manette, an innocent prisoner, denounce to the times when all these things shall be answered for. I denounce them to Heaven and to earth."

A terrible sound arose when the reading of the Doctor's letter was done. Charles Darnay was the son and nephew of those evil nobles. He and his family had been denounced by the man whose daughter he had later married. At every juryman's vote, there was a roar. Unanimously voted. An aristocrat by descent; and, therefore, an enemy of the Republic. Darnay was sentenced to die within twenty-four hours.

The doomed prisoner was allowed to speak with Lucie a

moment. "Farewell, darling of my soul. My parting blessing on my love." Then Charles stretched out his hand to Doctor Manette: "We know now what you underwent when you learned my name Evrémonde. I know the natural hatred you conquered for my sake and Lucie's. I thank you with all my heart."

Lucie fainted and Sydney Carton carried her outside, where Mr. Lorry was waiting with a carriage. When they arrived at the apartment, Carton carried Lucie to a couch, kissed her, saying, "A life you love," and left.

He walked to Defarge's wineshop, took a seat, and ordered wine, taking care to seem unschooled in the French language. Sydney Carton listened closely as Madame Defarge argued loudly that Lucie, her child, and her father should be guillotined also. Carton also learned that Madame Defarge was the youngest daughter of the peasant family injured by the Evrémonde brothers.

Arriving back at Tellson's, Carton told Mr. Lorry of the grave danger that was present for Lucie, her child, and her father. Then he said, "Don't ask me why I make the rules I am going to make. I have a reason. This is the paper which enables me to pass out of this city. You see — Sydney Carton, an Englishman! Keep it for me until tomorrow. Doctor Manette has similar papers for his daughter, her child and himself. Collect them for safekeeping and have your horses ready at two o'clock tomorrow afternoon.

"Quietly have all these arrangements made, even to the taking of your own seat in the carriage. The moment I come to you, take me in, and drive away. Wait for nothing but to have my place filled, and then for England! Change the course, or delay in it," Carton said, "and no life can possibly be saved."

THE GUILLOTINE

7

"This is the day of my death!" thought Charles Darnay as the light of dawn arrived. He passed the morning hours walking to and fro in his prison cell. At one o'clock he heard footsteps outside the door and Sydney Carton entered.

"You are not," Charles said with a worried look, "a prisoner?"

"You have no time to ask why or what my being here means," said Carton. "Simply do as I say. Take off your boots and draw on these of mine. Quick!"

"Carton, there is no escaping from this place. You will only die with me."

"I do not ask you to escape. Now, change that cravat and coat for mine. Shake your hair out like mine."

"Carton, I beg you not to add your death to the bitterness of mine."

Ignoring Darnay's pleas, Carton said, "Take this pen and paper and write what I dictate. Quick, friend, quick!"

"If you remember," Carton dictated and Charles wrote, "the words that passed between us long ago, you will understand this message."

Charles looked up and saw Carton's hand stop inside his shirt and close upon something. Carton continued to dictate:

"I am thankful that the time has come when I can prove them. That I do so is no subject for regret or grief." As Carton spoke, his hand, with the packets from the chemist's shop, slowly moved close to the writer's face. Darnay felt dizzy as he breathed in some sort of gas.

The pen dropped from Darnay's fingers and Carton saw that Charles' writing had trailed off into unintelligible signs. Charles sprang up with a reproachful look and for a few seconds struggled with the man who had come to lay down his life for him. Then he fainted away.

Carton quickly dressed himself in the clothes Charles had laid aside. Then he softly called, "Enter, there!" and the spy Barsad appeared as Carton was putting the written paper in Charles' shirt.

"Now, get help and take me to the coach," Carton told Barsad.

"You?" said Barsad nervously.

"Him, man, with whom I have exchanged. I was weak and faint when you brought me in, and I am fainter now you take me out."

The spy left and returned with two men, who lifted the unconscious figure, and carried it away. The door closed and Carton was left alone.

When the clock struck two the jailer arrived. "Follow me, Evrémonde!" he said, and the prisoner followed.

The bleak, wintery, afternoon shadows which fell on the prison were also on a coach which was stopped at the gate to the city. Papers were handed out and read.

"Alexandre Manette. Physician. French. Lucie. His daughter. French. Sydney Carton. Advocate. English. Which is he?"

"He lies here in the corner of carriage," said Mr. Lorry.

"Apparently the English advocate is in a swoon?" said the guard.

"It is hoped he will recover in the fresher air."

"Jarvis Lorry. Banker. English. Which is he?"

Mr. Lorry answered, "I am he;" the guard signed their papers and the carriage passed through the gate.

Along the Paris streets, screaming crowds had assembled to watch the daily executions. Crash! A head was held up and the knitting women counted twenty-one. Sydney Carton — the supposed Evrémonde — stood calmly as the women counted twenty-two.

"I am the resurrection and the life; saith the Lord; he that believeth in me, though he were dead, yet shall he live . . . "

The murmuring of many voices, the upturning of many faces, all flashed away. Twenty-three. They said of him, that it was the peacefullest man's face ever beheld there.

The truth was that before his death, Sydney Carton had a vision in which the evil in France gradually wore itself out. He saw in his vision that he lived in the memories of the Darnay family, who would name a son after him. The son would become an honest and successful judge, thereby fulfilling Carton's own unfulfilled ambitions.

Peace came with Sydney Carton's dying words: "It is a far, far better thing that I do, than I have ever done; it is a far, far better rest that I go to, than I have ever known."

GLOSSARY

aristocrat (ə ris′ tə krat) a person who is born into a high social position

chateau (sha tō′) a large country house

cockade (kä kād′) a small badge worn in the hat

denounce (di nàuns′) to speak out against someone or something in public

dictate (dik′ tāt′) to say something aloud for someone else to write down

emigrant (em′ i grənt) someone who leaves his or her own country to live somewhere else

execution (ek′ sə kyü′ shən) the act of putting someone to death by a legal order

guillotine (gil′ ə tēn) a machine for cutting off a person's head with a sharp blade

patriot (pā′ trē ət) a person who loves and supports his or her country

treason (trēz′ ən) the act of turning against your own country to help its enemies